Grover Cleveland

Fishing and Shooting Sketches

outlook

Grover Cleveland

Fishing and Shooting Sketches

1st Edition | ISBN: 978-3-73403-521-0

Place of Publication: Frankfurt am Main, Germany

Year of Publication: 2018

Outlook Verlag GmbH, Deutschland.

Reproduction of the original.

Fishing and Shooting Sketches

BY

GROVER CLEVELAND

Illustrated by
HENRY S. WATSON

NEW YORK
THE OUTING PUBLISHING COMPANY
1906

Copyright, 1901, 1902, 1903, 1904, by The Curtis Publishing Co.
Copyright, 1903, 1904, 1905, 1906, by The Independent.
Copyright, 1903, by The Press Publishing Co.
Copyright, 1905, by The Country Calendar.

Copyright, 1906, by The Outing Publishing Company.

Entered at Stationers' Hall, London, England.

All Rights Reserved.

THE OUTING PRESS
DEPOSIT, N. Y.

From Copyright Photo, by Pach.

The Mission of Sport & Out Door Life.

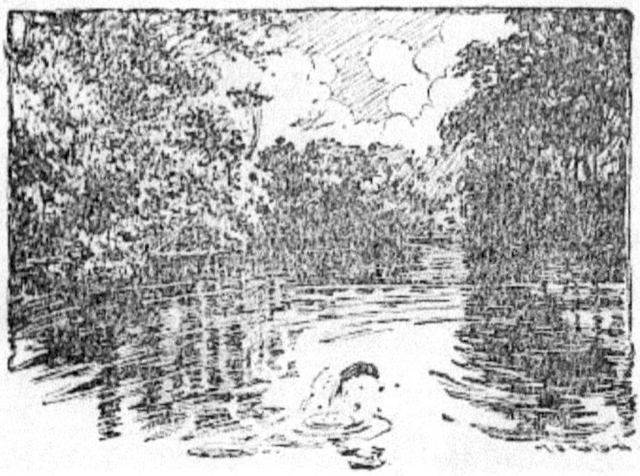

The Mission of Sport and Outdoor Life

I am sure that it is not necessary for me, at this late day, to dwell upon the fact that I am an enthusiast in my devotion to hunting and fishing, as well as every other kind of outdoor recreation. I am so proud of this devotion that, although my sporting proclivities have at times subjected me to criticism and petty forms of persecution, I make no claim that my steadfastness should be looked upon as manifesting the courage of martyrdom. On the contrary, I regard these criticisms and persecutions as nothing more serious than gnat stings suffered on the bank of a stream—vexations to be borne with patience and afterward easily submerged in the memory of abundant delightful accompaniments. Thus, when short fishing excursions, in which I have sought relief from the wearing labors and perplexities of official duty, have been denounced in a mendacious newspaper as dishonest devices to cover scandalous revelry, I have been able to enjoy a sort of pleasurable contempt for the author of this accusation, while congratulating myself on the mental and physical restoration I had derived from these excursions. So, also, when people, more mistaken than malicious, have wagged their heads in pitying fashion and deprecated my indulgence in hunting and fishing frivolity, which, in high public service, I have found it easy to lament the neglect of these amiable persons to accumulate for their delectation a fund of charming sporting reminiscence; while, at the same time, I sadly reflected how their dispositions might have been sweetened and their lives made happier if they had yielded something to the particular type of frivolity which they deplored.

I hope it may not be amiss for me to supplement these personal observations by the direct confession that, so far as my attachment to outdoor sports may be considered a fault, I am, as related to this especial predicament of guilt, utterly incorrigible and shameless. Not many years ago, while residing in a non-sporting but delightfully cultured and refined community, I found that considerable indignation had been aroused among certain good neighbors and friends, because it had been said of me that I was willing to associate in the field with any loafer who was the owner of a dog and gun. I am sure that I did not in the least undervalue the extreme friendliness of those inclined to intervene in my defense; and yet, at the risk of doing an apparently ungracious thing, I felt inexorably constrained to check their kindly efforts by promptly conceding that the charge was too nearly true to be denied.

There can be no doubt that certain men are endowed with a sort of inherent and spontaneous instinct which leads them to hunting and fishing indulgence as the most alluring and satisfying of all recreations. In this view, I believe it may be safely said that the true hunter or fisherman is born, not made. I believe, too, that those who thus by instinct and birthright belong to the sporting fraternity and are actuated by a genuine sporting spirit, are neither cruel, nor greedy and wasteful of the game and fish they pursue; and I am convinced that there can be no better conservators of the sensible and provident protection of game and fish than those who are enthusiastic in their pursuit, but who, at the same time, are regulated and restrained by the sort of chivalric fairness and generosity, felt and recognized by every true sportsman.

While it is most agreeable thus to consider hunting and fishing as constituting, for those especially endowed for their enjoyment, the most tempting of outdoor sports, it is easily apparent that there is a practical value to these sports as well as all other outdoor recreations, which rests upon a broader foundation. Though the delightful and passionate love for outdoor sports and recreation is not bestowed upon every one as a natural gift, they are so palpably related to health and vigor, and so inseparably connected with the work of life and comfort of existence, that it is happily ordained that a desire or a willingness for their enjoyment may be cultivated to an extent sufficient to meet the requirements of health and self-care. In other words, all but the absolutely indifferent can be made to realize that outdoor air and activity, intimacy with nature and acquaintanceship with birds and animals and fish, are essential to physical and mental strength, under the exactions of an unescapable decree.

Men may accumulate wealth in neglect of the law of recreation; but how infinitely much they will forfeit, in the deprivation of wholesome vigor, in the loss of the placid fitness for the quiet joys and comforts of advancing years, and in the displacement of contented age by the demon of querulous and premature decrepitude!

> "For the good God who loveth us
> He made and loveth all."

A Law not to Be Disobeyed

Men, in disobedience of this law, may achieve triumph in the world of science, education and art; but how unsatisfying are the rewards thus gained if they hasten the night when no man can work, and if the later hours of life are haunted by futile regrets for what is still left undone, that might have been done if there had been closer communion with nature's visible forms!

In addition to the delight which outdoor recreations afford to those instinctively in harmony with their enjoyment, and after a recognition of the fact that a knowledge of their nerve- and muscle-saving ministrations may be sensibly cultivated, there still remains another large item that should be placed to their credit. Every individual, as a unit in the scheme of civilized social life, owes to every man, woman and child within such relationship an uninterrupted contribution to the fund of enlivening and pleasurable social intercourse. None of us can deny this obligation; and none of us can discharge it as we ought, if our contributions are made in the questionable coin of sordidness and nature's perversion. Our experience and observation supply abundant proof that those who contribute most generously to the exhilaration and charm of social intercourse will be found among the disciples of outdoor recreation, who are in touch with nature and have thus kept fresh and unperverted a simple love of humanity's best environment.

A Chance in the Open for All

It seems to me that thoughtful men should not be accused of exaggerated fears when they deprecate the wealth-mad rush and struggle of American life and the consequent neglect of outdoor recreation, with the impairment of that mental and physical vigor absolutely essential to our national welfare, and so abundantly promised to those who gratefully recognize, in nature's adjustment to the wants of man, the care of "the good God" who "made and loveth all."

Manifestly, if outdoor recreations are important to the individual and to the nation, and if there is danger of their neglect, every instrumentality should be heartily encouraged which aims to create and stimulate their indulgence in every form.

Fortunately, the field is broad and furnishes a choice for all except those wilfully at fault. The sky and sun above the head, the soil beneath the feet, and outdoor air on every side are the indispensable requisites.

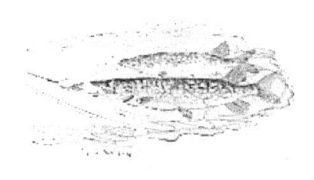

A Defence of Fishermen.

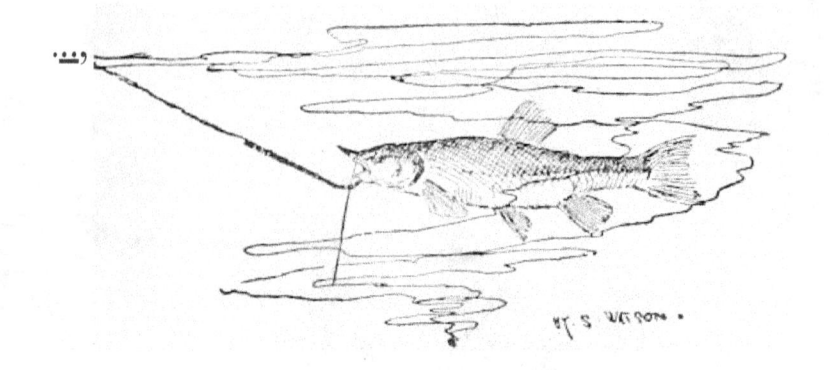

A Defense of Fishermen

By way of introduction and explanation, it should be said that there is no intention at this time to deal with those who fish for a livelihood. Those sturdy and hard-working people need no vindication or defense. Our concern is with those who fish because they have an occult and mysterious instinct which leads them to love it, because they court the healthful, invigorating exertion it invites, and because its indulgence brings them in close contact and communion with Nature's best and most elevating manifestations. This sort of fishing is pleasure and not work—sport and not money-grabbing. Therefore it is contemptuously regarded in certain quarters as no better than a waste of time.

Generous fishermen cannot fail to look with pity upon the benighted persons who have no better conception than this of the uses and beneficent objects of rational diversion. In these sad and ominous days of mad fortune-chasing, every patriotic, thoughtful citizen, whether he fishes or not, should lament that we have not among our countrymen more fishermen. There can be no doubt that the promise of industrial peace, of contented labor and of healthful moderation in the pursuit of wealth, in this democratic country of ours, would be infinitely improved if a large share of the time which has been devoted to the concoction of trust and business combinations, had been spent in fishing.

The narrow and ill-conditioned people who snarlingly count all fishermen as belonging to the lazy and good-for-nothing class, and who take satisfaction in describing an angler's outfit as a contrivance with a hook at one end and a fool at the other, have been so thoroughly discredited that no one could wish for their more irredeemable submersion. Statesmen, judges, clergymen, lawyers and doctors, as well as thousands of other outspoken members of the fishing fraternity, have so effectively given the lie to these revilers of an honest and conscientious brotherhood that a large majority have been glad to find refuge in ignominious silence.

Notwithstanding this, weak, piping voices are still occasionally heard accusing fishermen of certain shortcomings and faults. These are so unsubstantial and unimportant that, as against the high place in the world's esteem claimed by those who love to fish, they might well be regarded as non-essentials, or, in a phrase of the day, as mere matters of detail. But, although it may be true that these charges are on the merits unworthy of notice, it cannot be expected that fishermen, proud of the name, will be amiably willing to permit those making such accusations the satisfaction of remaining unchallenged.

The Hangers-on of the Fraternity

At the outset, the fact should be recognized that the community of fishermen constitute a separate class or a sub-race among the inhabitants of the earth. It has sometimes been said that fishermen cannot be manufactured. This is true to the extent that nothing can supply the lack of certain inherent, constitutional and inborn qualities or traits which are absolutely necessary to a fisherman's make-up. Of course there are many who call themselves fishermen and who insist upon their membership in the fraternity who have not in their veins a drop of legitimate fisherman blood. Their self-asserted relationship is nevertheless sometimes seized upon by malicious or ignorant critics as permitting the assumption that the weaknesses and sins of these pretenders are the weaknesses and sins of genuine fishermen; but in truth these pretenders are only interlopers who have learned a little fish language, who love to fish only "when they bite," who whine at bad luck, who betray incredulity when they hear a rousing fish story, and who do or leave undone many other things fatal to good and regular standing. They are like certain whites called squaw-men, who hang about Indian reservations, and gain certain advantages in the tribes by marrying full-blooded Indian women. Surely no just person would for a moment suppose that genuine Indians could be treated fairly by measuring them according to a squaw-man standard. Neither can genuine fishermen be fairly treated by judging them according to the standards presented by squaw-fishermen.

In point of fact, full-blooded fishermen whose title is clear, and whose natural qualifications are undisputed, have ideas, habits of thought and mental tendencies so peculiarly and especially their own, and their beliefs and code of ethics are so exclusively fitted to their needs and surroundings, that an attempt on the part of strangers to speak or write concerning the character or conduct of its approved membership savors of impudent presumption. None but fishermen can properly deal with these delicate matters.

What sense is there in the charge of laziness sometimes made against true fishermen? Laziness has no place in the constitution of a man who starts at sunrise and tramps all day with only a sandwich to eat, floundering through bushes and briers and stumbling over rocks or wading streams in pursuit of the elusive trout. Neither can a fisherman who, with rod in hand, sits in a boat or on a bank all day be called lazy—provided he attends to his fishing and is physically and mentally alert in his occupation. This charge may perhaps be truthfully made against squaw-fishermen who become easily discouraged, who "tire and faint" early, and lie down under the shade to sleep, or go in swimming, or who gaze about or read a book while their hooks rest baitless on the bottom; but how false and unfair it is to accuse regular, full-blooded fishermen of laziness, based on such performances as these! And yet this is absurdly done by those who cannot tell a reel from a compass, and who by way of familiarizing themselves with their topic leave their beds at eight o'clock in the morning, ride to an office at ten, sit at a desk until three or perhaps five, with an hour's interval for a hearty luncheon, and go home in the proud belief that they have done an active, hard day's work. Fishermen find no fault with what they do in their own affairs, nor with their conception of work; but they do insist that such people have no right to impute laziness to those who fish.

Why Fish Stories Should Be Believed

It is sometimes said that there is such close relationship between mendacity and fishing, that in matters connected with their craft all fishermen are untruthful. It must, of course, be admitted that large stories of fishing adventure are sometimes told by fishermen—and why should this not be so? Beyond all question there is no sphere of human activity so full of strange and wonderful incidents as theirs. Fish are constantly doing the most mysterious and startling things; and no one has yet been wise enough to explain their ways or account for their conduct. The best fishermen do not attempt it; they move and strive in the atmosphere of mystery and uncertainty, constantly aiming to reach results without a clue, and through the cultivation of faculties, non-existent or inoperative in the common mind.

In these circumstances fishermen necessarily see and do wonderful things. If those not members of the brotherhood are unable to assimilate the recital of these wonders, it is because their believing apparatus has not been properly regulated and stimulated. Such disability falls very far short of justifying doubt as to the truth of the narration. The things narrated have been seen and experienced with a fisherman's eyes and perceptions. This is perfectly understood by listening fishermen; and they, to their enjoyment and edification, are permitted by a properly adjusted mental equipment to believe what they hear.

This faculty is one of the safest signs of full-blooded right to membership. If incredulity is intimated by a professional member no injustice will be done if he is at once put under suspicion as a squaw-fisherman. As to non-members who accuse true fishermen of falsehood, it is perfectly clear that they are utterly unfitted to deal with the subject. The only theory fitting the condition leads to the statement that any story of personal experience told by a fisherman is to the fishing apprehension indubitably true; and that since disbelief in other quarters is owing to the lack of this apprehension, the folly of accusing fishermen of habitual untruthfulness is quite apparent.

The Taking of the Leviathan

The position thus taken by the brotherhood requires that they stand solidly together in all circumstances. Tarpon fishing has added greatly to our responsibilities. Even larger fish than these may, with the extension of American possessions, fall within the treatment of American fishermen. As in all past emergencies, we shall be found sufficient in such future exigencies. All will go well if, without a pretense of benevolent assimilation, we still fish as is our wont, and continue our belief in all that our brethren declare they have done or can do. A few thousand years ago the question was impressively asked, "Canst thou draw out leviathan with a hook?" We must not falter, if, upon its repetition in the future, a brother replies: "Yes, with a ten-ounce rod;" nor must we be staggered even if another declares he has already landed one of these monsters. If American institutions are found adequate to the new tasks which Destiny has put upon them in the extension of our lands, the American Chapter of the world's fishermen must not fail by their time-honored methods and practices, and by such truthfulness as belongs to the fraternity in the narration of fishing adventure, to subdue any new difficulties presented by the extension of our waters.

Why the Biggest Fish Are Always Lost

Before leaving this branch of our subject, especial reference should be made to one item more conspicuous, perhaps, than any other, among those comprised in the general charge of fishermen's mendacity. It is constantly said that they greatly exaggerate the size of the fish that are lost. This accusation, though most frequently and flippantly made, is in point of fact based upon the most absurd arrogance and a love of slanderous assertion that passes understanding. These are harsh words; but they are abundantly justified.

In the first place, all the presumptions are with the fisherman's contention. It is perfectly plain that large fish are more apt to escape than small ones. Of course their weight and activity, combined with the increased trickiness and resourcefulness of age and experience, greatly increase their ability to tear out the hook, and enhance the danger that their antics will expose a fatal weakness in hook, leader, line or rod. Another presumption which must be regretfully mentioned, arises from the fact that in many cases the encounter with a large fish causes such excitement, and such distraction or perversion of judgment, on the part of the fisherman as leads him to do the wrong thing or fail to do the right thing at the critical instant—thus actually and effectively contributing to an escape which could not and would not have occurred except in favor of a large fish.

Beyond these presumptions we have the deliberate and simple story of the fisherman himself, giving with the utmost sincerity all the details of his misfortune, and indicating the length of the fish he has lost, or giving in pounds his exact weight. Now, why should this statement be discredited? It is made by one who struggled with the escaped fish. Perhaps he saw it. This, however, is not important, for he certainly felt it on his rod, and he knows precisely how his rod behaves in the emergency of every conceivable strain.

The Finny Hypnotist

All true fishermen who listen to his plain, unvarnished tale accept with absolute faith the declared length and weight of the fish that was almost caught; but with every presumption, besides positive statement, against them, carping outsiders who cannot fish, and who love to accuse fishermen of lying, are exposed in an attempt to originate or perpetuate an envious and malicious libel.

The case of our fraternity on this point of absolute and exact truthfulness is capable of such irrefragable demonstration that anything in the way of confession and avoidance ought to be considered inadmissible. And yet, simply for the sake of argument, or by way of curious speculation, it may be interesting to intimate how a variation of a few inches in the exact length or a few ounces in the exact weight of a lost fish, as given by the loser, may be accounted for, without meanly attributing to him intentional falsehood. The theory has been recently started, that a trained hunting dog points a bird in the field solely because the bird's scent creates a hypnotic influence on the dog, which impels him by a sort of suggestion to direct his nose toward the spot from which such scent emanates. If there is anything worth considering in this theory, why may not a struggling fish at the end of a line exert such a hypnotic influence on the intensely excited and receptive nature at the other extremity of the fishing outfit, as to suggest an arbitrary and independent statement of the dimensions of the hypnotizer?

With the accusations already mentioned it would certainly seem that the enmity of those who take pleasure in reviling fishermen and their ways should be satisfied. They have not been content, however, in the demonstration of their evil-mindedness without adding to their indictment against the brotherhood the charge of profanity. Of course, they have not the hardihood to allege that our profanity is of that habitual and low sort which characterizes the coarse and ill-bred, who offend all decent people by constantly interlarding their speech with fearful and irrelevant oaths. They, nevertheless, find sufficient excuse for their accusation in the sudden ejaculations, outwardly resembling profanity, which are occasionally wrung from fishermen in trying crises and in moments of soul-straining unkindness of Fate.

Now, this question of profanity is largely one of intention and deliberation. The man who, intending what he says, coolly indulges in imprecation, is guilty of an offense that admits of no excuse or extenuation; but a fisherman can hardly be called profane who, when overtaken without warning by disaster, and abruptly hurled from the exhilarating heights of delightful anticipation to the depths of dire disappointment, impulsively gives vent to his pent-up emotion by the use of a word which, though found in the list of oaths, is spoken without intentional imprecation, and because nothing else seems to suit the occasion. It is by no means to be admitted that fishing tends even to this semblance of profanity. On the contrary, it imposes a self-restraint and patient forbearance upon its advanced devotees which tend to prevent sudden outbursts of feeling.

It must in frankness be admitted, however, by fishermen of every degree, that when the largest trout of the day, after a long struggle, winds the leader about a snag and escapes, or when a large salmon or bass, apparently fatigued to the point of non-resistance, suddenly, by an unexpected and vicious leap, frees himself from the hook, the fisherman's code of morals will not condemn beyond forgiveness the holder of the straightened rod if he impulsively, but with all the gentility at his command, exclaims: "Damn that fish!" It is probably better not to speak at all; but if strong words are to be used, perhaps these will serve as well as any that can do justice to the occasion.

Uncle Toby, overcome with tender sympathy, swore with an unctious, rotund oath, that his sick friend should not die; and we are told that "the accusing spirit which flew up to Heaven's chancery with the oath blushed as he gave it in; and the recording angel as he wrote it down dropped a tear upon the word and blotted it out forever."

The defense of the fishing fraternity which has been here attempted is by no means as completely stated as it should be. Nor should the world be allowed to overlook the admirable affirmative qualities which exist among genuine members of the brotherhood, and the useful traits which an indulgence in the gentle art cultivates and fosters. A recital of these, with a description of the personal peculiarities found in the ranks of fishermen, and the influence of these peculiarities on success or failure, are necessary to a thorough vindication of those who worthily illustrate the virtues of our clan.

The Serene Duck Hunter.

The Serene Duck Hunter

In the estimation of many people, all those who for any purpose or in any manner hunt ducks are grouped together and indiscriminately called duck hunters. This is a very superficial way of dealing with an important subject. In point of fact, the objects of duck shooting and its methods of enjoyment are so various, and the disposition and personal characteristics of those who engage in it present such strong contrasts, that a recognition of their differences should suggest the subdivision of this group into distinct and well-defined sections. Such a subdivision would undoubtedly promote fairness and justice, and lead to a better understanding of the general topic.

There are those whose only claim to a place among duck hunters is based upon the fact that they shoot ducks for the market. No duck is safe from their pursuit in any place, either by day or night. Not a particle of sportsmanlike spirit enters into this pursuit, and the idea never enters their minds that a duck has any rights that a hunter is bound to respect. The killing they do amounts to bald assassination—to murder for the sake of money. All fair-minded men must agree that duck hunters of this sort should be segregated from all others and placed in a section by themselves. They are the market shooters.

There are others claiming a place in the duck-hunting group, who, though not so murderously inclined as the market shooters, have such peculiar traits and such distinctive habits of thought and action, as abundantly justify placing them also in a classification of their own. These are the hunters who rarely miss a duck, but whose deadly aim affords them gratification only in so far as it is a prelude to duck mortality, and who are happy or discontented as their heap of dead is large or small. They have smothered the keen delights of imagination which should be the cheering concomitants of the most reputable grade of duck hunting, and have surrendered its pleasures to actual results and the force of external circumstances. Their stories of inordinate killing are frequently heard, and often enliven the pages of sporting magazines. There can be but little doubt that this contingent give unintentional support to a popular belief, originating in the market shooters' operations, that duck shooting is a relentlessly bloody affair. These are the dead shots among duck hunters.

The Vindication of the Gentle Huntsmen

The danger that all those who essay to shoot ducks may, by the conduct of these two classes, acquire a general and unmitigated reputation for persistent slaughter, cannot be contemplated without sadness. It is therefore not particularly reassuring to recall the fact that our countrymen seem just now to be especially attracted by the recital of incidents that involve killing,—whether it be the killing of men or any other living thing.

It is quite probable that the aggregation of all duck hunters in one general group cannot be at once remedied; and the expectation can hardly be entertained that any sub-classification now proposed will gain the acceptance and notoriety necessary for the immediate exoneration of those included within this group who are not in the least responsible for the sordid and sanguinary behavior of either the market shooter or the dead shot. These innocent ones comprise an undoubted majority of all duck hunters; and their common tastes and enjoyments, as well as their identical conceptions of duty and obligation, have drawn them together in delightful fraternity. By their moderate destruction of duck life they so modify the killing done by those belonging to the classes already described, that the aggregate, when distributed among the entire body of duck hunters, is relieved from the appearance of bloodthirsty carnage; and they in every way exert a wholesome influence in the direction of securing a place for duck hunting among recreations which are rational, exhilarating and only moderately fatal.

The Honorable Order of Serene Duck Hunters

It must be frankly confessed that the members of this fraternity cannot claim the ability to kill ducks as often as is required by the highest averages. This, however, does not in the least disturb their serenity. Their compensations are ample. They are saved from the sordid and hardening effects induced by habitual killing, and find pleasure in the cultivation of the more delicate and elevating susceptibilities which ducking environments should invite. Under the influence of these susceptibilities there is developed a pleasing and innocent self-deception, which induces the belief on the part of those with whom it has lodgment, that both abundant shooting skill and a thorough familiarity with all that pertains to the theory of duck hunting are entirely in their possession and control. They are also led to the stimulation of reciprocal credulity which seasons and makes digestible tales of ducking adventure. Nor does bloody activity distract their attention from their obligations to each other as members of their especial brotherhood, or cause them to overlook the rule which requires them to stand solidly together in the promotion and protection, at all hazards, of the shooting reputation of every one of their associates. These may well be called the Serene Duck Hunters.

All that has been thus far written may properly be regarded as merely an introduction to a description, somewhat in detail, of the manner in which these representatives of the best and most attractive type of duck hunters enjoy their favorite recreation.

A common and easy illustration of their indulgence of the sentimental enjoyments available to them is presented when members of the fraternity in the comfortable surroundings of camp undertake the discussion of the merits of guns and ammunition. The impressiveness with which guns are put to the shoulder with a view of discovering how they "come up," the comments on the length and "drop" of the different stocks, the solemn look through the barrel from the opened breech, and the suggestion of slight "pitting," are intensely interesting and gratifying to all concerned.

When these things are supplemented by an exchange of opinions concerning ammunition, a large contribution is added to the entertainment of the party. Such words as Schultz, Blue Ribbon, Dupont, Ballistite and Hazard are rolled like sweet morsels under the tongue. Each of the company declares his choice of powder and warmly defends its superiority, each announces the number of drams that a ducking cartridge should contain, and each declares his clear conviction touching the size of shot, and the amount, in ounces and fractions of ounces, that should constitute an effective load.

Undoubtedly the enjoyment supplied by such a discussion is keen and exhilarating. That it has the advantage of ease and convenience in its favor, is indicated by the fact that its effects are none the less real and penetrating in the entire absence of any knowledge of the topics discussed. To the serene duck hunter the pretense of knowledge or information is sufficient. The important factors in the affair are that each should have his turn, and should be attentively heard in his exploitation of that which he thinks he knows.

There is nothing in all this that can furnish reasonable ground for reproach or criticism. If under the sanction of harmless self-deception and pretense this duck-hunting contingent, to whom duck killing is not inevitably available, are content to look for enjoyment among the things more or less intimately related to it, it is quite their own affair. At any rate it is sufficient to say that they have joined the serene brotherhood for their pastime, and that any outside dictation or criticism of the mode in which they shall innocently enjoy their privileges of membership savors of gross impertinence.

There comes a time, however, when the calm and easy enjoyments of in-door comfort must give way to sterner activities, and when even the serene duck hunter must face the discomfort of severe weather and the responsibility of flying ducks. This exigency brings with it new duties and new objects of endeavor; but the principles which are characteristic of the fraternity are of universal application. Therefore our serene duck hunter should go forth resolved to accomplish the best results within his reach, but doubly resolved that in this new phase of his enjoyment he will betray no ignorance of any detail, and that he will fully avail himself of the rule unreservedly recognized in the brotherhood, which permits him to claim that every duck at which his gun is fired is hit—except in rare cases of conceded missing, when an excuse should be always ready, absolutely excluding any suggestion of bad shooting. And by way of showing his familiarity with the affair in hand it is not at all amiss for him to give some directions as he enters his blind as to the arrangement of the decoys.

How to Take Good and Bad Luck

It is quite likely that his first opportunity to shoot will be presented when a single duck hovers over the decoys, and as it poises itself offers as easy a target as if sitting on a fence. Our hunter's gun is coolly and gracefully raised, and simultaneously with its discharge the duck falls helplessly into the water. This is a situation that calls for no word to be spoken. Merely a self-satisfied and an almost indifferent expression of countenance should indicate that only the expected has happened, and that duck killing is to be the order of the day.

Perhaps after a reasonable wait, another venturesome duck will enter the zone of danger and pass with steady flight over the decoys easily within shooting distance. Again the gun of our serene hunter gives voice, summoning the bird to instant death. To an impartial observer, however, such a course would not seem to be in accordance with the duck's arrangements. This is plainly indicated by such an acceleration of flight as would naturally follow the noise of the gun's discharge and the whistling of the shot in the rear of the expected victim.

This is the moment when the man behind the gun should rise to the occasion, and under the rule governing the case should without the least delay or hesitation insist that the duck is hit. This may be done by the use of one of several appropriate exclamations—all having the sanction of precedent and long use. One which is quite clear and emphatic is to the effect that the fleeing duck is "lead ballasted," another easily understood is that it has "got a dose," and still another of no uncertain meaning, that it is "full of shot." Whatever particular formula is used, it should at once be followed by a decided command to the guide in attendance to watch the disappearing bird and mark where it falls.

The fact should be here mentioned that the complete enjoyment of this proceeding depends largely upon the tact and intelligence of the guide. If with these he has a due appreciation of his responsibility as an adjunct to the sport, and is also in proper accord with his principal, he will give ready support to the claim that the duck is mortally wounded, at the same time shrewdly and with apparent depression suggesting the improbability of recovering the slain.

If as the hours wear away this process becomes so monotonous as to be fatiguing, a restful variety may be introduced by guardedly acknowledging an occasional miss, and bringing into play the excuses and explanations appropriate to such altered conditions. A very useful way of accounting for a shot missed is by the suggestion that through a slightly erroneous calculation of distance the duck was out of range when the shot was fired. A very frequent and rather gratifying pretext for avoiding chagrin in case of a long shot missed is found in the claim that, though the sound of shot striking the bird is distinctly heard, their penetration is ineffective. Sometimes failure is attributed to the towering or turning of the duck at the instant of the gun's discharge. It is at times useful to impute failure to the probability that the particular cartridge used was stale and weak; and when all these are inadmissible, the small size of the shot and the faulty quality or quantity of powder they contain, may be made to do service; and, in extreme cases, their entire construction as well as their constructor may be roundly cursed as causes for a miscarriage of fatal results.

How True Duck Hunters Stand Together

When the ducks have ceased to fly for the day the serene duck hunter returns to camp in a tranquil, satisfied frame of mind befitting his fraternity membership. He has several ducks actually in hand, and he has fully enjoyed the self-deception and pretense which have led him to the belief that he has shot well. His few confessed misses are all satisfactorily accounted for; and he is too well broken to the vicissitudes of duck shooting, and too old a hunter, to be cast down by the bad fortune which has thickly scattered, over distant waters and marshes, his unrecovered dead.

When at the close of such a day a party of serene duck hunters are gathered together, a common fund of adventure is made up. Each as he contributes his share is entitled to add such embellishments of the imagination as will make his recital most interesting to his associates and gratifying to himself; and a law tacitly adopted but universally recognized by the company binds them all to an unquestioning acceptance of the truth of every narration. The successes of the day as well as its incidents of hard luck, and every excuse and explanation in mitigation of small returns of game, as they are rehearsed, create lively interest and quiet enjoyment. The one thing that might be a discordant note would be a hint or confession of downright and inexcusably bad shooting.

In this delightful assemblage of serene duck hunters there is no place for envious feeling toward either the slaughtering market shooter or the insatiable dead shot. They only seek, in their own mild and gentle way, the indulgence of the pleasures which the less bloody phases of duck hunting afford; and no censorious critic has the right to demand that their enjoyment should be marred or diminished by the exactions of veracity or self-abasement.

Reference has already been made to the scrupulous care of this fraternity for the promotion and preservation, at all hazards, of the shooting reputation of all the associates. This is a most important duty. Indeed, it may be reasonably feared that any neglect or faltering in its discharge would undermine the entire fabric of the serene brotherhood's renown. The outside world should never gain from any of its members the least hint that a weak spot has been developed in the shooting ability of any of their number; and in giving an account of hunting results it is quite within bounds for them to include in the aggregate, not only the ducks actually killed and those reported killed, but those probably killed and neither recovered nor reported. The fact that such an aggregate has been reported by an associate should impart to every member absolute verity, and each should make the statement his own, to the displacement of all other knowledge. Such ready support of each other's allegations and such entire self-abnegation are absolutely necessary if the safety of the organization is to be insured, and if its success and usefulness are to endure.

Thus the great body of serene duck hunters, who have associated together for the promotion of high aims and purposes, pursue the even tenor of their way. They do not clamor for noisy recognition or make cheap exhibition of their virtues. They will, however, steadily and unostentatiously persevere, both by precept and practice, in their mission to make all duck hunters better and happier, and to mitigate the harsh and bloody features of duck hunting.

The Mission of Fishing & Fishermen.

The Mission of Fishing and Fishermen

It was quite a long time ago that a compelling sense of duty led me to undertake the exoneration of a noble fraternity, of which I am an humble member, from certain narrow-minded, if not malicious, accusations. The title given to what was then written, "A Defense of Fishermen," was precisely descriptive of its purpose. It was not easy, however, to keep entirely within defensive limits; for the temptation was very strong and constant to abandon negation and palliation for the more pleasing task of commending to the admiration and affection of mankind in affirmative terms both fishing and fishermen. A determination to attempt this at another time, and thus supplement the matter then in hand, made resistance to this temptation successful; but the contemplated supplementation was then foreshadowed in the following terms:

> "The defense of the fishing fraternity which has been here attempted is by no means so completely stated as it should be. Nor should the world be allowed to overlook the admirable affirmative qualities which exist among genuine members of the brotherhood and the useful traits which the indulgence in the gentle art cultivates and fosters. A recital of these, with a description of the personal influence of these peculiarities found in the ranks of fishermen, and the influence of these peculiarities on success or failure, are necessary to a thorough vindication of those who worthily illustrate the virtues of our clan."

The execution of the design thus foreshadowed has until now been evaded on account of the importance and delicacy of the undertaking and a distrust of my ability to deal adequately with the subject. Though these misgivings have not been overcome, my perplexity, as I enter upon the work so long delayed, is somewhat relieved by the hope that true fishermen will be tolerant, whatever may be the measure of my success, and that all others concerned will be teachable and open-minded.

Lessons the Fisherman Learns from Nature

The plan I have laid out for the treatment of my topic leads me, first of all, to speak of the manner in which the fishing habit operates upon man's nature for its betterment; and afterward to deal with the qualities of heart and disposition necessary to the maintenance of good and regular standing in the fishing fraternity.

There is no man in the world capable of profitable thought who does not know that the real worth and genuineness of the human heart are measured by its readiness to submit to the influences of Nature, and to appreciate the goodness of the Supreme Power who has made and beautified Nature's abiding-place. In this domain, removed from the haunts of men and far away from the noise and dust of their turmoil and strife, the fishing that can fully delight the heart of the true fisherman is found; and here in its enjoyment, those who fish are led, consciously or unconsciously, to a quiet but distinct recognition of a power greater than man's, and a goodness far above human standards. Amid such surroundings and within such influences no true fisherman, whether sensitively attuned to sublime suggestion, or of a coarser mold and apparently intent only upon a successful catch, can fail to receive impressions which so elevate the soul and soften the heart as to make him a better man.

It is known of all men that one of the rudiments in the education of a true fisherman is the lesson of patience. If he has a natural tendency in this direction it must be cultivated. If such a tendency is lacking he must acquire patience by hard schooling. This quality is so indispensable in fishing circles that those who speak of a patient fisherman waste their words. In point of fact, and properly speaking, there can be no such thing as an impatient fisherman. It cannot, therefore, be denied that in so far as fishing is a teacher of the virtue of patience, it ought to be given a large item of credit in reckoning its relation to the everyday affairs of life; for certainly the potency of patience as a factor in all worldly achievements and progress cannot be overestimated. If faith can move mountains, patience and faith combined ought to move the universe.

Moreover, if those who fish must be patient, no one should fail to see that patience is a most desirable national trait and that it is vastly important to our body politic that there should continue among our people a large contingent of well-equipped fishermen, constantly prepared and willing to contribute to their country's fund of blessings a liberal and pure supply of this saving virtue.

To those who are satisfied with a superficial view of the subject it may seem impossible that the diligence and attention necessary to a fisherman's success can leave him any opportunity, while fishing, to thoughtfully contemplate any matter not related to his pursuit. Such a conception of the situation cannot be indorsed for a moment by those of us who are conversant with the mysterious and unaccountable mental phenomena which fishing develops. We know that the true fisherman finds no better time for profitable contemplation and mental exercise than when actually engaged with his angling outfit. It will probably never be possible for us to gather statistics showing the moving sermons, the enchanting poems, the learned arguments and eloquent orations that have been composed or constructed between the bites, strikes or rises of fish; but there can be no doubt that of the many intellectual triumphs won in every walk of life a larger proportion has been actually hooked and landed with a rod and reel by those of the fishing fraternity than have been secured in any one given condition of the non-fishing world.

This may appear to be a bold statement. It is intended as an assertion that fishing and fishermen have had much to do with the enlightenment and elevation of humanity. In support of this proposition volumes might be written; but only a brief array of near-at-hand evidence will be here presented.

Those who have been fortunate enough to hear the fervid eloquence of Henry Ward Beecher, and even those who have only read what he has written, cannot overlook his fishing propensity—so constantly manifest that the things he said and wrote were fairly redolent of fishing surroundings. His own specific confession of fealty was not needed to entitle him to the credentials of a true fisherman, nor to disclose one of the never-failing springs of his best inspiration. When these things are recalled, and when we contemplate the lofty mission so well performed by this noble angler, no member of our brotherhood can do better in its vindication than to point to his career as proof of what the fishing habit has done for humanity.

What Mashpee Waters Did for Webster

Daniel Webster, too, was a fisherman—always in good and regular standing. In marshaling the proof which his great life furnishes of the beneficence of the fishing propensity, I approach the task with a feeling of awe quite natural to one who has slept in the room occupied by the great Expounder during his fishing campaigns on Cape Cod and along the shores of Mashpee Pond and its adjacent streams. This distinguished member of our fraternity was an industrious and attentive fisherman. He was, besides, a wonderful orator—and largely so because he was a fisherman. He himself has confessed to the aid he received from a fishing environment in the preparation of his best oratorical efforts; and other irrefutable testimony to the same effect is at hand.

It is not deemed necessary to cite in proof of such aid more than a single incident. Perhaps none of Mr. Webster's orations was more notable, or added more to his lasting fame, than that delivered at the laying of the cornerstone of the Bunker Hill Monument. And it will probably be conceded that its most impressive and beautiful passage was addressed to the survivors of the War of Independence then present, beginning with the words, "Venerable men!" This thrilling oratorical flight was composed and elaborated by Mr. Webster while wading waist deep and casting his flies in Mashpee waters. He himself afterward often referred to this circumstance; and one who was his companion on this particular occasion has recorded the fact that, noticing indications of laxity in fishing action on Mr. Webster's part, he approached him, and that, in the exact words of this witness, "he seemed to be gazing at the overhanging trees, and presently advancing one foot and extending his right hand he commenced to speak, 'Venerable Men!'"

Mr. Webster's Remarks to a Fish

Though this should be enough to support conclusively the contention that incidents of Mr. Webster's great achievements prove the close relationship between fishing and the loftiest attainments of mankind, this branch of our subject ought not to be dismissed without reference to a conversation I once had with old John Attaquin, then a patriarch among the few survivors of the Mashpee Indians. He had often been Mr. Webster's guide and companion on his fishing trips and remembered clearly many of their happenings. It was with a glow of love and admiration amounting almost to worship that he related how this great fisherman, after landing a large trout on the bank of the stream, "talked mighty strong and fine to that fish and told him what a mistake he had made, and what a fool he was to take that fly, and that he would have been all right if he had let it alone." Who can doubt that patient search would disclose, somewhere in Mr. Webster's speeches and writings, the elaboration, with high intent, of that "mighty strong and fine" talk addressed to the fish at Mashpee?

The impressive story of this simple, truthful old Indian was delightfully continued when, with the enthusiasm of an untutored mind remembering pleasant sensations, the narrator told how the great fisherman and orator having concluded his "strong, fine talk," would frequently suit the action to the word, when he turned to his guide and proposed a fitting libation in recognition of his catch. This part of the story is not here repeated on account of its superior value as an addition to the evidence we have already gathered, but I am thus given an opportunity to speak of the emotion which fascinated me as the story proceeded, and as I recalled how precisely a certain souvenir called "the Webster Flask," carefully hoarded among my valued possessions, was fitted to the situation described.

Let it be distinctly understood that the claim is not here made that all who fish can become as great as Henry Ward Beecher or Daniel Webster. It is insisted, however, that fishing is a constructive force, capable of adding to and developing the best there is in any man who fishes in a proper spirit and among favorable surroundings. In other words, it is claimed that upon the evidence adduced it is impossible to avoid the conclusion that the fishing habit, by promoting close association with Nature, by teaching patience, and by generating or stimulating useful contemplation, tends directly to the increase of the intellectual power of its votaries, and, through them, to the improvement of our national character.

In pursuance of the plan adopted for the presentation of our subject, mention must now be made of the qualities of heart and disposition absolutely essential to the maintenance of honorable membership in the fishing fraternity. This mode of procedure is not only made necessary by the exigencies of our scheme, but the brotherhood of fishermen would not be satisfied if the exploitation of their service to humanity and their value to the country should terminate with a recital of the usefulness of their honorable pursuit. The record would be woefully incomplete if reference were omitted to the relation of fishing to the moral characteristics and qualities of heart, with which it is as vitally connected as with the intellectual traits already mentioned.

No man can be a completely good fisherman unless within his piscatorial sphere he is generous, sympathetic and honest. If he expects to enjoy that hearty and unrestrained confidence of his brethren in the fraternity which alone can make his membership a comfort and a delight, he must be generous to the point of willingness to share his last leaders and flies, or any other items of his outfit, with any worthy fellow-fisherman who may be in need. The manifestation of littleness and crowding selfishness often condoned in other quarters, and the over-reaching conduct so generally permitted in business circles, are unpardonable crimes in the true fisherman's code.

Of course, there is nothing to prevent those from fishing who wholly disregard all rules of generosity, fairness and decency. Nor can we of the brotherhood of true fishermen always shield ourselves from the reproach to which we are subjected by those who steal our livery and disgrace it by casting aside all manly liberality in their intercourse with other fishermen and all considerate self-restraint in their intercourse with fish. We constantly deprecate the existence of those called by our name, in whose low conception of the subject, fishing is but a greedy game, where selfishness and meanness are the winning cards, and where the stakes are the indiscriminate and ruthless slaughter of fish; and let it be here said, once for all, that with these we have nothing to do except to condemn them as we pass. Our concern is with true fishermen—a very different type of mankind—and with those who *prima facie* have some claim to the title.

How to Know a True Fisherman

No burdensome qualifications or tedious probation obstruct the entrance to this fraternity; but skill and fishing ability count for nothing in eligibility. The oldest and most experienced and skillful fisherman will look with composure upon the vanishing chances of his catch through the floundering efforts of an awkward beginner, if the awkward flounderer has shown that he is sound at heart. He may not fish well, but if he does not deliberately rush ahead of all companions to pre-empt every promising place in the stream, nor everlastingly study to secure for his use the best of the bait, nor always fail to return borrowed tackle, nor prove to be blind, deaf and dumb when others are in tackle need, nor crowd into another's place, nor draw his flask in secrecy, nor light a cigar with no suggestion of another, nor do a score of other indefinable mean things that among true fishermen constitute him an unbearable nuisance, he will not only be tolerated but aided in every possible way.

It is curious to observe how inevitably the brotherhood discovers unworthiness. Even without an overt act it is detected—apparently by a sort of instinct. In any event, and in spite of the most cunning precautions, the sin of the unfit is sure to find them out; and no excuse is allowed to avert unforgiving ostracism as its punishment.

A true fisherman is conservative, provident, not given to envy, considerate of the rights of others, and careful of his good name. He fishes many a day and returns at night to his home, hungry, tired and disappointed; but he still has faith in his methods, and is not tempted to try new and more deadly lures. On the contrary, he is willing in all circumstances to give the fish the chance for life which a liberal sporting disposition has determined to be their due; and he will bide his time under old conditions. He will not indulge his fishing propensity to the extent of the wanton destruction and waste of fish; he will not envy the superior advantages of another in the indulgence of the pastime he loves so well; he will never be known to poach upon the preserves of a fortunate neighbor; and no one will be quicker or more spirited than he in the defense of his fishing honor and character.

Truth as Defined by the Honorable Guild

This detailed recital of the necessary qualifications of good fisherman-ship serves most importantly as the prelude of an invitation for skeptics to observe the complete identity of these qualifications with the factors necessary to good citizenship, and from thence to concede a more ready recognition of the honorable place which should be awarded to the fraternity among the agencies of our country's good.

In conclusion, and to the end that there should be no appearance of timidity or lack of frankness, something should be said explanatory of the degree and kind of truthfulness which an honorable standing in the fishing fraternity exacts. Of course, the notion must not be for a moment tolerated that deliberate, downright lying as to an essential matter is permissible. It must be confessed, however, that unescapable traditions and certain inexorable conditions of our brotherhood tend to a modification of the standards of truthfulness which have been set up in other quarters. Beyond doubt, our members should be as reliable in statement as our traditions and full enjoyment of fraternity membership will permit.

An attempt has been made to remedy the indefiniteness of this requirement by insisting that no statement should be regarded as sufficiently truthful for the fisherman's code that had not for its foundation at least a belief of its correctness on the part of the member making it. This was regarded as too much elasticity in the quality of the belief required. The matter seems to have been finally adjusted in a manner expressed in the motto: "In essentials— truthfulness; in non-essentials—reciprocal latitude." If it is objected that there may be great difficulty and perplexity in determining what are essentials and what non-essentials under this rule, it should be remembered that no human arrangements, especially those involving morals and ethics, can be made to fit all emergencies.

In any event, great comfort is to be found in the absolute certainty that the law of truthfulness will be so administered by the brotherhood that no one will ever be permitted to suffer in mind, body or estate by reason of fishermen's tales.

Some Fishing Pretenses & Affectations.

Some Fishing Pretenses and Affectations

I would not permit without a resentful protest an expression of doubt as to my good and regular standing in the best and most respectable circle of fishermen. I am as jealous as a man can be of the fair fame of the fraternity; and I am unyielding in my insistence upon the exclusion of the unworthy from its membership. I also accept without demur all the traditions of the order, provided that they have been always in the keeping of the faithful, and carefully protected against all discrediting incidents. In addition to all this, my faculty of credence has been so cultivated and strengthened that I yield without question implicit and unquestioning belief to every fishing story— provided always that it is told by a fisherman of good repute, and on his own responsibility. This is especially a matter of loyalty and principle with me, for I am not only convinced that the usefulness and perhaps the perpetuity of the order of Free and Accepted Fishermen depends upon a bland and trustful credulity in the intercourse of its members with each other, but I have constantly in mind the golden rule of our craft, which commands us to believe as we would be believed.

I have not made this profession of faith in a spirit of vainglorious conceit, but by way of indicating the standpoint from which I shall venture to comment on some weaknesses which afflict our brotherhood, and as a reminder that the place I have earned among my associates should in fairness and decency protect me from the least accusation of censoriousness or purposeless faultfinding.

I do not propose to make charges of wickedness and wrong-doing, which call for such radical corrective treatment as might imperil the peace and brotherly love of our organization. It is rather my intention mildly to criticise some affectations and pretenses which I believe have grown out of overtraining among fishermen, or have resulted from too much elaboration of method and refinement of theory.

These affectations and pretenses are, unfortunately, accompaniments of a high grade of fishing skill; and in certain influential quarters they are not only excused but openly and stoutly justified. I cannot, therefore, expect my characterization of them as faults and weaknesses to pass unchallenged; but I hope that in discharging the duty I have undertaken I shall not incur the unfriendship of any considerable number of my fishing brethren.

It has often occurred to me that the very noticeable and increasing tendency toward effeminate attenuation and æsthetic standards among anglers of an advanced type, is calculated to bring about a substitution of scientific display with rod and reel for the plain, downright, common-sense enjoyment of fishing. This would be a distinct and lamentable loss, resulting in the elimination to a great extent of individual initiative, and the disregard of the inherent distinction between good and bad fishermen, as measured by natural aptitude and practical results.

As in an organized commonwealth neither the highest nor the lowest elements of its people constitute its best strength and reliance, so in the fraternity of fishermen neither the lowest hangers-on and intruders, nor the highest theorists who would make fishing a scientific exercise instead of a manly, recreative pursuit, make up the supporting and defensive power of the organization. It is the middle class in the community of fishermen, those who fish sensibly and decently, though they may be oblivious to the advantages of carrying fishing refinements far beyond the exigencies of catching fish, upon whom we must depend for the promotion and protection of the practical interests of the brotherhood.

It is, therefore, of the utmost importance that the zeal and enthusiasm of this valuable section of our membership should not be imperiled by subjecting them to the humiliating consciousness that their sterling fishing qualities are held in only patronizing toleration by those in the fraternity who gratuitously assume fictitious and unjustifiable superiority.

I shall attempt to locate the responsibility for the affectations and pretenses I have mentioned, not only in vindication of our sincere and well-intentioned rank and file, but for another reason, which concerns the peace of mind and comfort of every member of the organization in his relationship with the outside world. The fact that we are in a manner separated from the common mass of mankind naturally arouses the unfriendly jealousy of those beyond the pale of the brotherhood; and fishing—the fundamental object and purpose of our union—is in many quarters decried as an absurd exertion or a frivolous waste of time. In such circumstances we cannot be charged with a surrender of independence if we attempt by a frank statement to deprive these ill-natured critics of all excuse for attacking our entire body on account of faults and weaknesses for which only a small minority is responsible.

Bluntly stated, the affectations and pretenses which I have in mind, and which in my opinion threaten to bring injury upon our noble pursuit, grow out of the undue prominence and exaggerated superiority claimed for fly-casting for trout. I hasten to say for myself and on behalf of all well-conditioned fishermen that we are not inclined to disparage in the least the delightful exhilaration of the sudden rise and strike, nor the pleasurable exercise of skill and deft manipulation afforded by this method of fishing. We have no desire to disturb by a discordant dissent the extravagant praise awarded to the trout when he is called the wariest of his tribe, "the speckled beauty," the aristocratic gentleman among fish, and the most toothsome of his species. At the same time, we of the unpretentious sort of fishermen are not obliged to forget that often the trout will refuse to rise or strike and will wait on the bottom for food like any plebeian fish, that he is frequently unwary and stupid enough to be lured to his death by casts of the fly that are no better than the most awkward flings, that notwithstanding his fine dress and aristocratic bearing it is not unusual to find him in very low company, that this gentleman among fish is a willing and shameless cannibal, and that his toothsomeness, not extraordinary at best, is probably more dependent than that of most fish upon his surroundings.

While our knowledge of these things does not exact from us an independent protest against constantly repeated praise of the qualities of trout and of fly-casting as a means of taking them, it perhaps adds to the spirit and emphasis of our dissent when we are told that fly-casting for trout is the only style of fishing worthy of cultivation, and that no other method ought to be undertaken by a true fisherman. This is one of the deplorable fishing affectations and pretenses which the sensible rank and file of the fraternity ought openly to expose and repudiate. Our irritation is greatly increased when we recall the fact that every one of these super-refined fly-casting dictators, when he fails to allure trout by his most scientific casts, will chase grasshoppers to the point of profuse perspiration, and turn over logs and stones with feverish anxiety in quest of worms and grubs, if haply he can with these save himself from empty-handedness. Neither his fine theories nor his exclusive faith in fly-casting so develops his self-denying heroism that he will turn his back upon fat and lazy trout that will not rise.

We hear a great deal about long casts and the wonderful skill they require. To cast a fly well certainly demands dexterity and careful practice. It is a matter of nice manipulation, and a slight variation in execution is often apt to settle the question of success or failure in results. It is, besides, the most showy of all fishing accomplishments, and taken all together it is worth the best efforts and ambition of any fisherman. Inasmuch, however, as the tremendously long casts we hear of are merely exhibition performances and of but little if any practical use in the actual taking of fish, their exploitation may be classed among the rather harmless fishing affectations. There is a very different degree of rankness in the claim sometimes made that an expert caster can effectively send his fly on its distant mission by a motion of his forearm alone, while all above the elbow is strapped to his side. We take no risk in saying that such a thing was never done on a fishing excursion, and that the proposition in all its aspects is the baldest kind of a pretense.

As becomes a consistent member of the fraternity of fishermen, I have carefully avoided unfriendly accusation in dealing with a branch of fishing enthusiastically preferred by a considerable contingent of my associates. If, in lamenting the faddishness that has grown up about it, plain language has been used, I have nevertheless been as tolerant as the situation permits. No attempt has been made to gain the applause of pin-hook-and-sapling fishermen, nor to give the least comfort to those who are fishermen only in their own conceit, and whose coarse-handed awkwardness, even with the most approved tackle, leads them to be incurably envious of all those who fish well.

It is not pleasant to criticise, even in a mild way, anything that genuine fishermen may do—especially when their faults result from over-zealous attachment to one of the most prominent and attractive features of our craft's pursuit. It is, therefore, a relief to pass from the field of criticism, and in the best of humor, to set against the claim of exclusive merit made in behalf of fly-casting for trout the delights and compensations of black-bass fishing. I am sure I shall be seconded in this by a very large body of fishermen in the best of standing. It is manifestly proper also to select for this competition with trout casting a kind of fishing which presents a contrast in being uninfluenced by any affectations or by a particle of manufactured and fictitious inflation.

In speaking of black bass I am not dealing with the large-mouthed variety that are found in both Northern and Southern waters, and which grow in the latter to a very large size, but only with the small-mouthed family inhabiting the streams or lakes and ponds of the North, and which are large when they reach four pounds in weight. I consider these, when found in natural and favorable surroundings, more uncertain, whimsical and wary in biting, and more strong, resolute and resourceful when hooked, than any other fish ordinarily caught in fresh waters. They will in some localities and at certain seasons rise to a fly;

but this cannot be relied upon. They can sometimes also be taken by trolling; but this is very often not successful, and is at best a second-class style of fishing. On the whole it is best and most satisfactory to attempt their capture by still fishing with bait.

To those with experience this will not suggest angling of a tame and unruffled sort; and if those without experience have such an estimate of it they are most decidedly reckoning without their host. As teachers of patience in fishing, black bass are at the head of the list. They are so whimsical that the angler never knows whether on a certain day they will take small live fish, worms, frogs, crickets, grasshoppers, crawfish or some other outlandish bait; and he soon learns that in the most favorable conditions of wind and weather they will frequently refuse to touch bait of any kind. In their intercourse with fishermen, especially those in the early stages of proficiency, they are the most aggravating and profanity-provoking animal that swims in fresh water. Whether they will bite or not at any particular time we must freely concede is exclusively their own affair; but having decided this question against the fishermen, nothing but inherent and tantalizing meanness can account for the manner in which a black bass will even then rush for the bait, and after actually mouthing it will turn about and insultingly whack it with his tail. An angler who has seen this performance finds, in his desire to make things even with such unmannerly wretches, a motive in addition to all others for a relentless pursuit of the bass family.

Another and more encouraging stage in bass fishing is reached when biting seems to be the order of the day. It must not be supposed, however, that thereupon the angler's troubles and perplexities are over, or that nothing stands in the way of an easy and satisfying catch. Experience in this kind of fishing never fails to teach that it is one thing to induce these cunning fellows to take the bait, and quite another to accomplish their capture. It is absolutely necessary in this stage of the proceedings that the deliberation and gingerly touch of the fish be matched by the deliberation and care on the part of the fisherman at the butt of the rod; and the strike on his part must not be too much hastened, lest he fail to lodge his hook in a good holding place. Even if he succeeds in well hooking his fish he cannot confidently expect a certain capture. In point of fact the tension and anxiety of the work in hand begins at that very instant.

Ordinarily when a bass is struck with the hook, if he is in surroundings favorable to his activity, he at once enters upon a series of acrobatic performances which, during their continuance, keep the fisherman in a state of acute suspense. While he rushes away from and toward and around and under the boat, and while he is leaping from the water and turning somersaults with ugly shakes of his head, in efforts to dislodge the hook, there is at the other end of the outfit a fisherman, tortured by the fear of infirmity lurking somewhere in his tackle, and wrought to the point of distress by the thought of a light hook hold in the fish's jaw, and its liability to tear out in the struggle. If in the midst of it all a sudden release of pull and a straightening of his rod give the signal that the bass has won the battle, the vanquished angler has, after a short period of bad behavior and language, the questionable satisfaction of attempting to solve a forever unsolvable problem, by studying how his defeat might have been avoided if he had managed differently.

No such perplexing question, however, is presented to the bass fisherman who lands his fish. He complacently regards his triumph as the natural and expected result of steadiness and skill, and excludes from his thoughts all shadow of doubt concerning the complete correctness of his procedure in every detail.

My expressed design to place fishing for black bass with bait in competition with fly-casting for trout will, I hope, be considered a justification for the details I have given of bass fishing. It commends itself in every feature to the sporting instincts of all genuine anglers; and it is because I do not hope to altogether correct the "Affectations and Pretenses of Fishing" that I have felt constrained to rally those who should love angling for bass—to the end that at least a good-natured division may be established within our fraternity between an ornamental and pretense-breeding method and one which cultivates skill, stimulates the best fishing traits, and remains untouched by any form of affectation.

Summer Shooting.

Summer Shooting

As a general rule our guns should be put away for a long rest before the summer vacation. There is, however, one game situation which justifies their use, and it is this situation which sometimes appropriately allows a small-gauge gun to be placed beside the rod and reel in making up a vacation outfit.

In July or August the summer migration from their breeding places in the far North brings shore-birds and plover—both old and full-grown young—along our Eastern coast, in first-rate condition. My experience in shooting this game has all been within recent years, and almost entirely in the marshes and along the shores of Cape Cod. Like other members of the present generation and later comers in a limited field, I have been obliged to hear with tiresome iteration the old, old story of gray-haired men who tell of the "arms and the man" who in days gone by, on this identical ground, have slain these birds by thousands. The embellishment of these tales by all the incidents that mark the progress of our people in game extermination I have accepted as furnishing an explanation of the meager success of many of my excursions; but at the same time my condemnation of the methods of the inconsiderate slaughterers who preceded me has led to a consoling consciousness of my own superior sporting virtues.

While I am willing to confess to considerable resentment against those who in their shooting days were thoughtless enough to forget that I was to come after them, it must by no means be understood that my gunning for shore-birds has been discouraging. I have made some fair bags, and any bag is large enough for me, providing I have lost no opportunities and have shot well. Besides, I have never indulged in any shooting so conducive to the stimulation and strengthening of the incomparable virtue of patience. I have sat in a blind for five hours, by the watch—and awake nearly all the time at that—without seeing or hearing a bird worth shooting.

It is, however, neither the killing of birds nor the cultivation of patience that has exacted my absolute submission to the fascination of shore-bird shooting on Cape Cod. It is hard to explain this fascination, but my notion is that it grows out of a conceited attempt to calculate the direction of the wind and other weather conditions over-night, the elaborate preparations for a daylight start, the uncertainties of the pursuit under any conditions, the hope, amounting almost to expectation, that notwithstanding this the wisdom and calculation expended in determining upon the trip will be vindicated, the delightful early morning drive to the grounds, the anticipation of a flight of birds every moment while there, and the final sustaining expectation of their arrival in any event just before night. The singular thing in my case is that if all goes wrong at last, and even if under the influence of fatigue and disappointment I resolve during the drive home in chill and darkness that the trip will not be repeated for many a long day, it is quite certain that within forty-eight hours I shall be again observing the weather and guessing what the direction of the wind will be the next morning, in contemplation of another start.

But some will say, how are the incidents of hope and expectation, or of preparation and calculation, which are common to all sporting excursions, made to account for this especial infatuation with shore-bird shooting? I shall answer this question as well as I can by suggesting that the difference is one of degree. In gunning for other game one knows, or thinks he knows, where it is or ought to be. The wind and weather, while not entirely ignored, usually have a subordinate place in preliminary calculation, and the pleasures of hope and expectation are kept within the limits of ability or luck in finding the game. On the other hand, the shore-bird hunter knows not the abiding place of his game. He knows that at times during certain summer months these birds pass southward in their long migration, but he cannot know whether they will keep far out at sea or will on some unknown day be driven by wind and weather to the shore for temporary rest and feeding, and thus give him his opportunity. Though the presence on marsh or shore of a few bird stragglers may put him on his guard, it must still remain a question whether the game in sufficient quantities to make good shooting is hundreds or thousands of miles away or in the neighborhood of the shooting grounds.

I believe the unusual contingencies of shore-bird shooting and the wider scope they give for hope and expectation, together with the manifold conditions which give abundant opportunity for self-conceit in calculating probabilities, account for its quality of exceptional fascination.

The sportsman who persists is apt occasionally to find a good number of birds about the grounds; and when that happens, if he is adequately equipped with good decoys, and the right spirit, and especially if he is able to call the birds, he will enjoy a variety of fine shooting. The initiated well understand the importance of the call, and they know that the best caller will get the most birds. The notes of shore-birds, though quite dissimilar, are in most cases easily imitated after a little practice, and a simply constructed contrivance which can be purchased at almost any sporting goods store will answer for all the game if properly used. The birds are usually heard before they are seen, and if their notes are answered naturally and not too vehemently or too often, they will soon be seen within shooting range, whether they are Black-Breasted Plover, Chicken Plover, Yellow Legs, Piping Plover, Curlew, Sanderlings or Grass Birds. Of course, no decent hunter allows them to alight before he shoots.

I would not advise the summer vacationist who lacks the genuine sporting spirit to pursue the shore-bird. Those who do so should not disgrace themselves by killing the handsome little sand-pipers or peeps too small to eat. It is better to go home with nothing killed than to feel the weight of a mean, unsportsmanlike act.

A Word Concerning Rabbit Hunting.

Concerning Rabbit Shooting

Some hunters there are, of the super-refined and dudish sort, who deny to the rabbit any position among legitimate game animals; and there are others who, while grudgingly admitting rabbits to the list, seem to think it necessary to excuse their concession by calling them hares. I regard all this as pure affectation and nonsense. I deem it not beneath my dignity and standing as a reputable gunner to write of the rabbit as an entirely suitable member of the game community; and in doing so I am not dealing with hares or any other thing except plain, little everyday plebeian rabbits—sometimes appropriately called "cotton-tails." Though they may be "defamed by every charlatan" among hunters of self-constituted high degree, and despised by thousands who know nothing of their game qualities, I am not ashamed of their pursuit; and I count it by no means bad skill to force them by a successful shot to a topsy-turvy pause when at their best speed.

These sly little fellows feed at night, and during the day they hide so closely in grass or among rocks and brush that it is seldom they can be seen when at rest. Of course, no decent man will shoot a rabbit while sitting, and I have known them to refuse to start for anything less than a kick or punch. When they do start, however, they demonstrate quite clearly that they have kept their feet in the best possible position for a spring and run. After such a start the rabbit must in fairness be given an abundant chance to gain full headway, and when he has traversed the necessary distance for this, and is at his fastest gait, the hunter that shoots him has good reason to be satisfied with his marksmanship. I once actually poked one up and he escaped unhurt, though four loads of shot were sent after him.

In the main, however, dogs must be relied upon for the real enjoyment and success of rabbit hunting. The fastest dogs are not the best, because they are apt to chase the rabbit so swiftly and closely that he quickly betakes himself to a hole or other safe shelter, instead of relying upon his running ability. The baying of three or four good dogs steadily following a little cotton-tail should be as exhilarating and as pleasant to ears attuned to the music as if the chase were for bigger game. As the music is heard more distinctly, the hunter is allowed to flatter himself that his acute judgment can determine the route of the approaching game and the precise point from which an advantageous shot can be secured. The self-satisfied conceit aroused by a fortunate guess concerning this important detail, especially if supplemented by a fatal shot, should permit the lucky gunner to enjoy as fully the complacent pleasurable persuasion that the entire achievement is due to his sagacity, keenness and skill as though the animal circumvented were a larger beast. In either case the hunter experiences the delight born of a well-fed sense of superiority and self-pride; and this, notwithstanding all attempts to keep it in the background, is the most gratifying factor in every sporting indulgence.

Some people speak slightingly of the rabbit's eating qualities. This must be an abject surrender to fad or fashion. At any rate it is exceedingly unjust to the cotton-tail; and one who can relish tender chicken and refuse to eat a nicely cooked rabbit is, I believe, a victim of unfounded prejudices.

Why, then, should not rabbit hunting, when honorably pursued, be given a respectable place among gunning activities? It certainly has every element of rational outdoor recreation. It ministers to the most exhilarating and healthful exercise; it furnishes saving relief from care and overwork; it is free from wantonness and inexcusable destruction of animal life, and, if luck favors, it gives play to innocent but gratifying self-conceit.

Let us remember, however, that if rabbit hunting is to be a manly outdoor recreation, entirely free from meanness, and a sport in which a true hunter can indulge without shame, the little cotton-tail must in all circumstances be given a fair chance for his life.

A Word to Fishermen.

A Word to Fishermen

Those of us who fish in a fair, well-bred and reasonable way, for the purpose of recreation and as a means of increasing the table pleasures of ourselves or our friends, may well regret the apparently unalterable decree which gives to all those who fish, under the spur of any motive—good, bad or indifferent—the name of fishermen. We certainly have nothing in common with those who fish for a livelihood, unless it be a desire to catch fish. We have, in point of fact, no closer relationship than this with the murderously inclined, whose only motive in fishing is to make large catches, and whose sole pleasure in the pursuit is the gratification of a greedy propensity. Nevertheless we, and those with whom we have so little sympathy, are by a sort of unavoidable law of gravitation classed together in the same fraternity, and called fishermen. Occasionally weak attempts have been made to classify the best of this fraternity under the name of Anglers, or some title of that kind, but such efforts have always failed. Even Izaak Walton could not change the current of human thought by calling his immortal book "The Compleat Angler." So it seems however much those who fish may differ in social standing, in disposition and character, in motive and ambition, and even in mode of operation, all must abide, to the end of the chapter, in the contemplation of the outside world, within the brotherhood called "Fishermen." Happily, however, this grouping of incongruous elements under a common name does not prevent those of us who properly appreciate the importance of upholding the respectability of decent fishing from coming to an agreement concerning certain causes of congratulation and certain rules of conduct.

We who claim to represent the highest fishing aspirations are sometimes inclined to complain on days when the fish refuse to bite. There can be no worse exhibition than this of an entire misconception of a wise arrangement for our benefit. We should always remember that we have about us on every side thousands of those who claim membership in the fishing fraternity, because, in a way, they love to fish when the fish bite—and only then. These are contented only when capture is constant, and their only conception of the pleasures of fishing rests upon uninterrupted slaughter. If we reflect for a moment upon the consequences of turning an army of fishermen like these loose upon fish that would bite every day and every hour, we shall see how nicely the vicissitudes of fishing have been adjusted, and how precisely and useful the fatal attack of discouraging bad luck selects its victims. If on days when we catch few or no fish we feel symptoms of disappointment, these should immediately give way to satisfaction when we remember how many spurious and discouraged fishermen are spending their time in hammocks or under trees or on golf fields instead of with fishing outfits, solely on account of just such unfavorable days. We have no assurance that if fish could be easily taken at all times the fishing waters within our reach would not be depopulated—a horrible thing to contemplate. Let it not be said that such considerations as these savor of uncharitableness and selfishness on our part. We are only recognizing the doctrine of the survival of the fittest as applied to fishermen, and claiming that these "fittest" should have the best chance.

What has been said naturally leads to the suggestion that consistency requires those of us who are right-minded fishermen to reasonably limit ourselves as to the number of fish we should take on favorable days. On no account should edible fish be caught in such quantities as to be wasted. By restraining ourselves in this matter we discourage in our own natures the growth of greed, we prevent wicked waste, we make it easier for us to bear the fall between decent good luck and bad luck, or no luck, and we make ourselves at all points better men and better fishermen.

We ought not to forget these things as we enter upon the pleasures of our summer's fishing. But in any event let us take with us when we go out good tackle, good bait, and plenty of patience. If the wind is in the South or West so much the better, but let's go, wherever the wind may be. If we catch fish we shall add zest to our recreation. If we catch none, we shall still have the outing and the recreation—more healthful and more enjoyable than can be gained in any other way.

A Duck Hunting Trip.

A Duck-Hunting Trip

It is not a pleasant thing for one who prides himself on his strict obedience to game laws to be accused of violating these laws whenever he hunts or fishes —and especially is it exasperating to be thus accused solely for the delectation or profit of some hungry and mendacious newspaper correspondent. It is not true that I was once arrested in Virginia for violation of the game laws, or for shooting without a license; nor was any complaint ever made against me; nor, so far as I know, was such a thing ever contemplated.

Sport Versus Slaughter

Equally false and mischievous, though not involving a violation of law, was the charge that a party of which I was a member killed five hundred ducks. Our shooting force on that expedition consisted of five gunners of various grades of hunting ability, including one who had not "fired a gun in twenty years," and another who could "do pretty well with a rifle, but didn't know much about a shotgun." We were shooting four days, but on only one of these days was our entire force engaged. There was not one in the party who would not have been ashamed of any complicity in the killing of five hundred ducks, within the time spent and in the circumstances surrounding us; nor is there one of the party who does not believe that, if the extermination of wild ducks is to be prevented, and if our grandchildren are to know anything about duck shooting, except as a matter of historical reading, stringent and intelligent laws for the preservation of this game must be supplemented and aided by an aggressive sentiment firmly held among decent ducking sportsmen, making it disgraceful to kill ducks for the purpose of boasting of a big bag, or for the mere sake of killing. Those who hunt ducks with no better motives than these, and who are restrained, in the absence of law, by nothing except the lack of opportunity to kill, are duck-slaughterers, who merit the contempt of the present generation and the curses of generations yet to come.

Our party killed about one hundred and twenty-five ducks. We ate as many as we cared to eat during our stay among the hunting marshes, and we brought enough home to eat on our own tables and to distribute among our friends. It seems to me that gunners who kill as many ducks as will answer all these purposes ought to be satisfied.

On the Cooking of Wild Ducks

And just here I want to suggest something which ought to greatly curtail the distribution of wild ducks among our friends. In households where no idea prevails of the difference between properly cooking a wild duck and one brought up in a barnyard, a complimentary gift of wild fowl is certainly of questionable advisability; for if these are cooked after the fashion prescribed for the domestic duck they will be so thoroughly discredited in the eating that the recipient of the gift will come near suspecting a practical joke, and the donor will be nearly guilty of waste.

In Virginia they have a very good law prohibiting duck shooting on Wednesdays and Saturdays, and of course on Sundays. These are called rest days. We arrived at the very comfortable club-house of the Back Bay Club, in Princess Anne County, about noon one Saturday, with weather very fair and quiet—too much so for good ducking. From the time of our arrival until very early Monday morning, besides eating and sleeping, we had nothing to do but to "get ready." It must not be supposed that those words only mean the settlement in our quarters and the preparation of guns, ammunition and other outfit. Many other things are necessary by way of stimulating interest and filling the minds of waiting gunners with lively anticipation and hope. Thus during the preparatory hours left to us our eyes were strained hundreds of times from every favorable point of observation in search of flying ducks; hundreds of times the question as to the most desirable shooting points was discussed, and thousands of times the wish was expressed that Monday, instead of being a "blue bird day," would present us with a good, stiff breeze from the right direction. The field of prediction was open to all of us, and none avoided it. A telling hit was made by the most self-satisfied weather-prophet of the party, who foretold an east wind at sundown, which promptly made its appearance on schedule time.

When we were roused out of bed at 4.30 o'clock that Monday morning we found our east wind still with us in pretty good volume, and although we all knew it was not in the most favorable quarter, and that the weather was too warm for the best shooting, it was with high hopes that we got into our boats and started in midnight darkness for our blinds. Whatever anticipation of good shooting I had indulged met with a severe reverse when I learned that my shooting companion and I were expected to kill ducks with our decoys placed to the windward of us. I warmly protested against this, declaring that I had never done such a thing in my life, and in the strongest language I objected to the arrangement; but all to no purpose.

As I expected, the ducks that were inclined to fly within our range, coming up the wind behind us, saw our blinds and us before they saw the decoys, and when we tried to turn and get a shot, a sudden flare or tower put them out of reach. As for fair decoying, they had no notion of such a thing. We killed a few ducks through much tribulation; but the irritation of knowing that many good opportunities had been lost by our improper location more than overbalanced all the satisfaction of our slight success. That my theory on the subject of windward decoys is correct was proved when on Thursday, with a west wind and decoys to the leeward, we killed at the same place more than twice as many ducks as we killed the first day. This was not because more came to us, but because they came in proper fashion.

On Having One's "Eye Wiped"

It was on this day that I once or twice had my "eye wiped," and I recall it even now with anything but satisfaction. It is a provoking thing to miss a fair shot, but to have your companion after you have had your chance knock down the bird by a long, hard shot makes one feel somewhat distressed. This we call "wiping the eye"; but I have always thought the sensation caused by this operation justified calling it "gouging the eye."

We left for home after one more very cold day spent in the blinds, with some good shooting. Every one of the party was enthusiastic in speaking of the pleasure our outing had afforded us, and all were outspoken in the hope that our experience might be repeated in the future.

Now, let it be observed that most prominent among the things that had occupied us and were thus delightfully remembered, and among the experiences desired again in the future, were the rigors and discomforts we had undergone in our shooting. So far as the good things and the comforts of the club-house itself entered into the enjoyment of our trip, it would be strange if they did not present great allurement; for nothing in the way of snug shelter and good eating and drinking was lacking. It is not so easy, however, to reason out the duck hunter's eagerness to leave a warm bed, morning after morning, long before light, and go shivering out into the cold and darkness for the sake of reaching his blind before daybreak—not to find there warmth and shelter, but to sit for hours chilled to the bone patiently waiting for the infrequent shot which reminds him that he is indulging in sport or healthful recreation. Suppose that such a regimen as this were prescribed in cold blood as necessary to health. How many would think health worth the cost of such hardships?

"The Duck Hunter Is Born—Not Made"

Suppose the discomforts willingly endured by duck hunters were required of employees in an industrial establishment. There would be one place where a condition of strike would be constant and chronic. If it be said that the gratification of bringing down ducks pays for all the suffering of their pursuit, the question obtrudes itself, how is this compensation forthcoming in the stress of bad luck or no luck, and how is it that the duck-hunting propensity survives all conditions and all fortunes?

I am satisfied that there is but one way to account for the unyielding enthusiasm of those who hunt ducks and for their steady devotion to their favorite recreation: The duck hunter is born—not made.

Quail Shooting.

Quail Shooting

We hear a great deal in these days about abundant physical exercise as a necessary factor in the maintenance of sound health and vigor. This is so universally and persistently enjoined upon us by those whose studies and efforts are devoted to our bodily welfare that frequently, if we withhold an iota of belief concerning any detail of the proposition, we subject ourselves to the accusation of recklessly discrediting the laws of health.

While beyond all doubt a wholesale denial of the importance of physical exertion to a desirable condition of bodily strength would savor of foolish hardihood, we are by no means obliged to concede that mere activity of muscles without accompaniment constitutes the exercise best calculated to do us good. In point of fact we are only boldly honest and sincere when we insist that really beneficial exercise consists as much in the pursuit of some independent object we desire to reach or gain by physical exertion, coupled with a pleasant stimulation of mental interest and recreation, as in any given kind or degree of mere muscular activity. Bodily movement alone, undertaken from a sense of duty or upon medical advice, is among the dreary and unsatisfying things of life. It may cultivate or increase animal strength and endurance, but it is apt at the same time to weaken and distort the disposition and temper. The medicine is not only distasteful, but fails in efficacy unless it is mingled with the agreeable and healing ingredients of mental recreation and desirable objects of endeavor.

I am convinced that nothing meets all the requirements of rational, healthful outdoor exercise more completely than quail shooting. It seems to be so compounded of wholesome things that it reaches, with vitalizing effect, every point of mental or physical enervation. Under the prohibitions of the law, or the restraints of sporting decency, or both, it is permitted only at a season of the year when nature freely dispenses, to those who submit to her treatment, the potent tonic of cool and bracing air and the invigorating influences of fields and trees and sky, no longer vexed by summer heat. It invites early rising; and as a general rule a successful search for these uncertain birds involves long miles of travel on foot. Obviously this sport furnishes an abundance of muscular action and physically strengthening surroundings. These, fortunately, are supplemented by the eager alertness essential to the discovery and capture of game well worth the effort, and by the recreative and self-satisfying complacency of more or less skillful shooting.

In addition to all this, the quail shooter has on his excursions a companion, who not only promotes his success, but whose manner of contributing to it is a constant source of delight. I am not speaking of human companionship, which frequently mars pleasure by insistent competition or awkward interference, but of the companionship of a faithful, devoted helper, never discouraged or discontented with his allotted service, except when the man behind the gun shoots badly, and always dumbly willing to concede to the shooter the entire credit of a successful hunt. The work in the field of a well-trained dog is of itself an exhibition abundantly worth the fatigue of a quailing expedition. It behooves the hunter, however, to remember that the dog is in the field for business, and that no amount of sentimental admiration of his performances on the part of his master will compensate him, if, after he has found and indicated the location of the game, it escapes through inattention or bad shooting at the critical instant. The careless or bungling shooter who repeatedly misses all manner of fair shots, must not be surprised if, in utter disgust, his dog companion sulkily ceases effort, or even wholly abandons the field, leaving the chagrined and disappointed hunter to return home alone—leg weary, gameless and ashamed. He is thus forced to learn that hunting-dog intelligence is not limited to abject subservience; and he thus gains a new appreciation of the fact that the better his dog, the better the shooter must know "what to do with his gun."

I do not assume to be competent to give instruction in quail shooting. I miss too often to undertake such a *rôle*. It may not, however, be entirely unprofitable to mention a fault which I suppose to be somewhat common among those who have not reached the point of satisfactory skill, and which my experience has taught me will stand in the way of success as long as it remains uncorrected. I refer to the instinctive and difficultly controlled impulse to shoot too quickly when the bird rises. The flight seems to be much more speedy than it really is; and the undrilled shooter, if he has any idea in his mind at all, is dominated by the fear that if the formality of aiming his gun is observed the game will be beyond range before he shoots. This leads to a nervous, flustered pointing of the gun in the direction of the bird's flight, and its discharge at such close range that the load of shot hardly separates in the intervening distance. Nine times out of ten the result is, of course, a complete miss; and if the bird should at any time under these conditions be accidentally hit, it would be difficult to find its scattered fragments. An old quail shooter once advised a younger one afflicted with this sort of quick triggeritis: "When the bird gets up, if you chew tobacco spit over your shoulder before you shoot."

It is absolutely certain that he who aspires to do good quail shooting must keep cool; and it is just as certain that he must trust the carrying qualities of his gun as well as his own ability and the intelligence of his dog. If he observes these rules, experience and practice will do the rest.

I hope I may be allowed to suggest that both those who appreciate the table qualities of the toothsome quail, and those who know the keen enjoyment and health-giving results of their pursuit, should recognize it as quite worth their while, and as a matter of duty, to co-operate in every movement having for its object the protection, preservation and propagation of this game. Our quail have many natural enemies; they are often decimated by the severity of winter, and there are human beings so degraded and so lost to shame as to seek their destruction in ways most foul. A covey of quail will sometimes huddle as close together as possible in a circle, with their heads turned outward. I have heard of men who, discovering them in this situation, have fired upon them, killing every one at a single shot. There ought to be a law which would consign one guilty of this crime to prison for a comfortable term of years. A story is told of a man so stupidly unsportsmanlike that when he was interfered with as he raised his gun, apparently to shoot a quail running on the ground, he exclaimed with irritation: "I did not intend to shoot until it had stopped running." This may be called innocent stupidity; but there is no place for such a man among sportsmen, and he is certainly out of place among quail.

It is cause for congratulation that so much has been done for quail protection and preservation through the enactment of laws for that purpose. But neither these nor their perfunctory enforcement will be sufficiently effective. There must be, in addition, an active sentiment aroused in support of more advanced game legislation, and of willing, voluntary service in aid of its enforcement; and in the meantime all belonging to the sporting fraternity should teach that genuine sportsmanship is based upon honor, generosity, obedience to law and a scrupulous willingness to perpetuate, for those who come after them, the recreation they themselves enjoy.

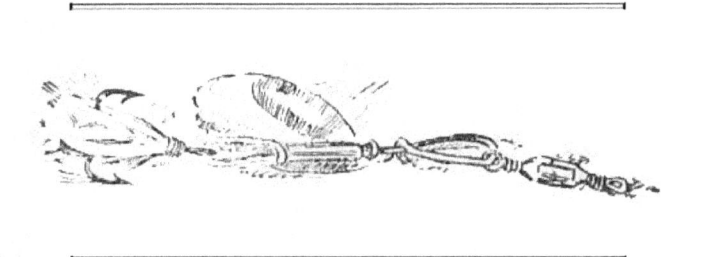

CPSIA information can be obtained
at www.ICGtesting.com
Printed in the USA
LVHW100741070622
720666LV00003B/80